This book belongs to

♥ .... ♥

Sandy Creek
387 Park Avenue South
New York, NY 10016

ISBN 978-1-4351-3314-3

10 9 8 7 6 5 4 3 2 Lot
Manufactured 02/07/2012
Printed in China

My Best Friend

Written by Gaby Goldsack ♥ Illustrated by Frances Evans

Sandy Creek

Emily was playing in the backyard
with her favorite doll, Hannah.

"Hello, Emily!" called a cheerful voice.
It was Sarah, who lived next door.
The two girls were best friends.

"Can I play with Hannah, too?" asked Sarah,
reaching out to pick her up.

Emily held on tightly to Hannah. She was
a very special doll, and Emily didn't like anybody
else to play with her.

"Hannah's tired," said Emily. "I think I'll put her to bed. Then I'll come back and play with you."

Sarah sighed. She'd really like to play with Hannah. Emily was so lucky to have such a beautiful doll.

For the rest of the morning, Emily and Sarah played
in Emily's yard. First they took turns pushing each other
on the swing to see who could go the highest.

Then they played in Emily's treehouse. It was *their* special hideout, and nobody else was allowed in it. They both thought it was great living next door to one another.

The next day, both girls got up early and ran down to the front yard. They were very excited. They were going on vacation together. Every year, they went to the same vacation cottage.

Sarah was traveling with Emily's
family. That way they could talk to each
other on the journey.

"Can Hannah sit between us?" she
asked Emily as they climbed into the car.

"Sorry," said Emily. "Hannah says she
wants to sit by the window." And she
tucked Hannah safely out of Sarah's reach.

At last they arrived at the cottage, and the girls raced from room to room checking that nothing had changed since last year.

At bedtime, they snuggled down in their cozy beds in the attic. They loved sharing a room on vacation. They stayed awake long after the lights went out, talking and laughing together.

This vacation was the best one yet. The sun shone
and Sarah and Emily spent most of their days playing
outside. One day Sarah rode her bicycle without training
wheels for the first time. The next day Emily did the same.

It always seemed to happen like that. One of the girls would learn something new, and then the other would quickly follow in her footsteps. Soon the girls were racing each other on their bikes. They played all day and had never been happier.

One sunny morning, Sarah and Emily went for
a pony ride. At the riding center, Emily was put on a
black pony called Buttons, and Sarah was put on
a dappled pony called Bonnie.

Full of excitement, Sarah and Emily were led round a small paddock by two older girls. When Buttons broke into a bumpy trot, Emily giggled with glee.

"Me too!" cried Sarah, and Bonnie trotted as well.

The two friends couldn't wait to tell their parents what a wonderful time they'd had.

"Can we go riding again when we get home?" Sarah asked her mom and dad. The girls' moms looked at each other and frowned.

"Hmmm," began Sarah's mom, "there's something we've been meaning to tell you. Things will be a little different when we get home." Sarah's mom and dad had something important to tell her.

Back at the cottage, Sarah's dad broke the news.

"We're moving away," he began. "I've got a new job, and Mommy and I have found a wonderful new house."

Emily and Sarah couldn't believe their ears. They wouldn't be neighbors anymore!

"It's not too far. You'll still be able to see Emily on weekends and during vacations," he said.

"But I don't want to move!" cried Sarah. She threw her arms around Emily. "You won't forget me, will you?" she whispered.

"No!" said Emily.

For the rest of the vacation, Sarah pleaded with her parents.

"Can't we stay at our old house?" she asked.

Sarah's dad tried to explain everything slowly and patiently. He told her that his new job was too far away to drive to each day.

"Emily can come and stay whenever she wants," he said.

"Can I go and stay with Emily sometimes, too?" Sarah asked her mom.

"Of course," her mom replied.

"And will I still be your best friend?" Sarah asked Emily.

"Of course," said Emily.

Back at home after the vacation, the last days of the summer flew by. Sarah watched sadly as all the things in her house were packed into boxes.

"Do you think Emily will forget me?" Sarah asked her mom.

"Of course not," replied her mom, giving her a comforting hug. "But just to make sure, why don't we buy her a special good-bye present?"

On the morning that Sarah and her family were due to leave, Emily and her parents gathered outside the house to say good-bye.

"I've brought you a present to remember me by," said Sarah, handing Emily the gift. Emily ripped off the paper. Nestled inside was a gorgeous golden heart necklace.

"It's beautiful!" Emily smiled. As she picked up the necklace, she suddenly noticed something.

"Look," she cried. "There are two chains with two pendants! You put them together to make a heart, and it says 'Best Friends'." She handed one to Sarah.

"You have one pendant, and then whenever you look at it you can think of me. That way, we will never really be apart."

At last the two friends realized that they could still be best friends even when they weren't next-door neighbors.

Just then, Emily rushed inside the house. She came out a minute later carrying Hannah.

"Here," she said, putting the doll into Sarah's arms. "Hannah will keep you company until you make friends at your new house."

Sarah was speechless. She gave Emily an enormous hug. She looked so happy that Emily knew she had done the right thing.

Emily held her pendant next to Sarah's and grinned. "Sharing really is great," she declared. "Especially sharing things with your very best friend."